1777
YEAR OF THE SEVENS

Mary Z. Holmes
Illustrated by Geri Strigenz

STONE
BANK
BOOKS

RAINTREE
STECK-VAUGHN
LIBRARY
Austin, Texas

* For Tom *

This text and art were reviewed for accuracy by William Dodd Brown, author of "The Capture of Daniel Boone's Saltmakers: Fresh Perspectives from Primary Sources" and "A Visit to Boonesborough in 1779: The Recollections of Pioneer George M. Bedinger," Chicago, IL.

Designed by Geri Strigenz

Published by Raintree/Steck-Vaughn Library
P.O. Box 26015, Austin, TX 78755

Library of Congress Cataloging-in-Publication Data
Holmes, Mary Z.
    Year of the sevens / Mary Z. Holmes ; illustrated by Geri Strigenz
       p. cm. — (History's children)
    "A Stone Bank Book"
    Summary: In 1777, thirteen-year-old Polly and her family face great danger after they move to the Kentucky frontier.
    ISBN 0-8114-3505-9. — ISBN 0-8114-6430-X (pbk.)
    1. Kentucky—History—Revolution. 1775-1783—Juvenile fiction. [1. Kentucky—History—Revolution, 1775-1783—Fiction. 2. United States—History—Revolution. 1775-1783—Fiction. 3. Frontier and pioneer life—Fiction.] I. Strigenz, Geri K., ill. II. Title. III. Series: Holmes, Mary Z. History's children.
PZ7.H7375Ye 1992   91-33190
[Fic]—dc20   CIP AC

Printed in the United States of America
1 2 3 4 5 6 7 8 9 WZ 96 95 94 93 92

1777

*T*his story takes place at the frontier fort of Harrodsburg, in what is now the state of Kentucky. In 1777, a handful of brave pioneers are living here. It is the time of the Revolutionary War. The American colonies are fighting the British for their independence.

The Kentucky people are alone in the wilderness. They are fighting too, far from the protection of the American armies. The British have sent the Indians to attack the small Kentucky settlements. It is a time of great danger for these pioneers.

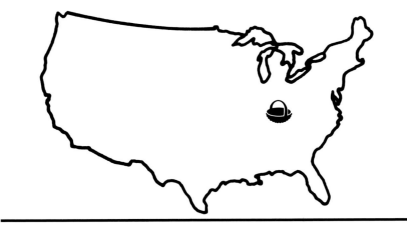

HISTORICAL PERSONAGES

The following people mentioned in this book really lived in Kentucky in the 1770s:

Daniel Boone

Jemima Boone

Simon Butler

Betsey Callaway

Colonel Callaway

Fanny Callaway

George Rogers Clark

William Coomes

Jane Coomes

James Harrod

John Hinkston

Mrs. Logan and baby William

John McClellan

James Ray

William Ray

Barney Stagner

I

KENTUCKY

My children have a strong liking for stories about my girl-hood. "Tell us about the year of the sevens," they beg me. They mean that awful year of 1777 when I was only thirteen. Lord have mercy on us, that was a mighty bad year. Back then we used to say, "Good times are coming, but we may never live to see them."

My six little ones sit before the fire and wait for me to begin. My oldest boy says that listening to me tell stories is like fishing. It takes a lot of waiting to get to the good part. "She'll start with 1774," he says, "like she always does."

They've heard the tale many times before.

* * *

Ma said that Pa had itching feet. By that she meant that Pa liked to travel. Staying in one place made him restless.

Back in 1774, Pa had us on a farm on the frontier of Pennsyl-vania. To the west, where our land ended, was the great forest. Pa would disappear into the forest to hunt or just to see what was out there. Sometimes, he was gone for a long time.

Ma said there were many folks living to the east, and that bothered Pa. He liked wild places better. Back east, there were more places like ours. Folks had built log cabins and cleared the

land to make fields just like we had. And Ma said there were towns even farther east. If you went far enough, you came to big towns along the Atlantic Ocean. But I never did see the towns or the ocean. All I knew was our land.

There were six of us living in the cabin. There was Pa, whose name was James McBee, and my mother Abby. Then there was me, Polly McBee, and my little brother Charley. That made four of us. The other two were Pa's brothers, Billy and Joe, who lived with us for as long as I can remember. Uncle Billy was always doing silly things and making a fool out of himself. Uncle Joe was sour. Folks said they never saw Joe crack a smile.

That year, 1774, Pa said he was going into the far country to the west. He felt it was getting too crowded where we were and he was thinking of moving on. I never saw many folks near our place, but Pa traveled, so I guess he knew if too many folks were settling nearby. Anyway, Pa was away for several months. When he returned, he told us he'd been to a faraway place called Kentucky. Pa had joined James Harrod and some other men to lay out a new settlement there.

"It's a paradise for sure," Pa said. "There are rivers, huge trees, and rich grasslands. It's filled with buffalo, deer, birds, and fish. And hardly any people at all," he said with a grin. "Only a few new settlers like us. That's where we'll be going."

Pa and Uncle Billy went off to Kentucky the next year to clear land and build a cabin. Uncle Joe stayed home to do the planting. By that time, folks had cleared some forest just beyond our place. Now we had neighbors. Pa was right about Pennsylvania getting crowded.

I asked Ma if she wanted to leave. "Kentucky sounds like a fine place," Ma told me. "Maybe I have itching feet too." I didn't tell her how I felt about going. I wanted to stay. This is where I was born. I loved it here.

Pa and Uncle Billy came back by the end of the summer, and we took some months to get ready for the move. Finally, in the spring of 1776, we left for Kentucky. Trying not to cry, I took a last look at my home. Then off we went with our horses, cows, hogs, and chickens. When we reached the Ohio River, Pa, Billy, and Joe built a flatboat for the animals and us. We packed Ma's kettles and things on the flatboat and set off down the river as fit as can be.

"We're going to Kentuck," Charley said. We had a hearty laugh at that because Charley hardly talked at all. He was only three or so at the time.

Pa said we were lucky to be leaving Pennsylvania. There was a great war coming. The British and the colonists had begun to fight each other. That's when I first heard Pa and my uncles talk about Lexington and Bunker Hill, the early battles of the war. Ma and I listened as we watched Charley so he wouldn't fall in the water.

Once, the flatboat hit a rock in the river and came to a surprising stop. All of us fell down, even the animals. One of the hogs tumbled into the water. Uncle Joe leaned over the side to try and reach the hog. He even gave his best hog call. The hog looked back at him and squealed, then it swam away.

Uncle Billy had a laughing fit. "Did you see the look on that hog's face?" he asked and slapped his leg. Uncle Joe wouldn't talk to any of us for two days.

After about a week, we pulled up at a place called Limestone Creek in Kentucky. There we met Simon Butler, who told us there were plenty other folks coming here this spring. He also said the Indians were being troublesome, so we should take care.

Pa hunted a turkey for us to eat. After resting a day and packing our things on the horses, we bid Mr. Butler good-bye and set off. We walked overland to our new place.

For a while, we followed a trail through the forest. Not even a grown man could get his arms around some of those tree trunks — they were so big. Then we came to great fields of cane, tall heavy grasses growing twice as high as Pa. We followed what seemed to be a wide road through the cane. Pa said it was a buffalo trace. The herds of buffalo had stomped down everything growing as they traveled their road again and again. It made a good road for folks too.

It took us quite a few days to complete our journey. We passed by little streams and springs as we moved on through the meadows, tall cane, and forests. We saw turkeys and squirrels and deer everywhere. The rivers were full of fish.

"I told you it was paradise," Pa said. But he was worried. At night, when we slept on the ground, he or Billy or Joe stayed awake to sit guard. They were watching for Indians.

We stopped off at the place where James Harrod's folks were working to build a fort. This is where Pa had come before. Harrodsburg had a number of cabins and three two-story blockhouses. The men were working on the stockade — a tall log fence that would go around the buildings. The blockhouses were at three of the corners of the fort. From the upper stories, men would be able to watch for Indians.

I saw other children, but felt too shy to speak to them. Charley, however, found a slave boy his age. They chased around and around us until Ma told them to go off and play somewhere else.

Since Pa was eager to get going, we didn't stay long at Harrodsburg. Our cabin was only a few miles away, down the Salt River.

"James McBee," Ma said when she saw the place, "you've done a heap of work here."

The cabin was all finished, and Pa and Uncle Billy had cut down trees to make a clearing in the forest. They'd even planted corn. Last year's crop still stood among the tree stumps in a cleared field. Pa opened the cabin and chased two raccoons out.

"Looks good," he said and led us into our new home. He pulled some boards from the small windows to let the light in. "Guess the McBees can be happy here?" he asked.

Ma smiled and said, "Oh my, yes." Then she got us all running. Uncle Joe and Uncle Billy unpacked the horses. Charley and I carried bundles into the cabin, and Pa went off to shoot a deer for our first meal.

It didn't take us long to settle in. In the days that followed, the weather warmed nicely, and Ma, Charley, and I put our shoes away for the summer. We got the dry corn out of the field and husked it. While Ma and I pounded the kernels down to cornmeal, the men planted new corn, turnips, and watermelons. Charley was in charge of planting the apple seeds brought from Pennsylvania.

As weeks passed, I couldn't help thinking about how things used to be. I missed my home in Pennsylvania. But I kept busy helping Ma milk the cows and feed the chickens, make soap, wash clothes, and cook.

One day Ma told me to come sit next to her before the stone fireplace. "You're a real good girl, Polly," she said. "I'm going to make you a new basket."

I sat and watched her sort out the thin splits of oak she would need. I always loved to watch her weave the splits around and around the basket frame. Ma made the prettiest baskets I ever did see.

She was the sweetest thing. That's what Pa said, and I agreed. Ma always had a smile for each one of us.

"I love you," I said to her.

Ma put her hand under my chin and looked into my eyes. "Oh, aren't you the one," she said. "I love you too, my girl."

She looked back to her work and started the basket. "I've been worried about you, Polly. You get so attached to things." Ma made two circles of oak and put them together to make the basket frame. "I was thinking you might leave your heart in Pennsylvania."

Ma always knew so much about me. She'd seen me taking that last long look at our old cabin. My powerful feelings were still there. The truth was, my heart wasn't in Kentucky.

"You've got to let go," Ma went on. "It's no good pining for what's in the past, is it?"

"No. But it's mighty hard sometimes, Ma."

Then she said, "Well, when this basket is done, you can put your heart in it." She smiled. "That way you'll have it right with you all the time."

I understood what she meant. Stop thinking about what was past. I should have my strong feelings with me in the present. I was soon to forget that lesson.

II

THE STOCKADE

Late in the summer of 1776, a man rode into our clearing. I recognized him right off as Simon Butler, the man we saw at Limestone Creek.

"How-de-do, McBee," he said to Pa.

"Howdy, Butler," Pa said. "What brings you here?"

Butler got off his horse. "I came to tell you the news. And if there's anyone here strong enough to lift a hunk of buffalo meat, there's some on the horse for you."

Uncle Billy laughed and lifted Butler up off the ground. "That strong enough for you?" he asked.

Ma came out of the cabin. "Land's sakes, Billy. Put him down and bring that meat inside. I'll cook it up."

Later, when the food was eaten, we sat in the cabin and listened to everything Simon Butler had to tell us.

"First the faraway news," he said. "I've heard tell from folks that we've declared our independence. Happened on July the fourth."

"What does that mean, Pa?" I asked.

"The colonies have said we don't belong to the British anymore," Pa told me. "But the British won't just let us go."

"It means a war to the end," Uncle Joe added in his sour way.

Pa shook his head. "Tell me, Butler, will the war reach us?"

"Can't say about the British," Butler said, "but I do have news about the Indians."

We held our breath.

"There was trouble over to Boonesborough in July," he started. This was another Kentucky settlement, only thirty-some miles away. "Some Cherokee and Shawnee took three girls. Boone and a bunch of fellows tracked them and managed to bring the girls back. No harm done."

"Who were the girls?" Ma asked him.

"Dan Boone's daughter, Jemima, and Colonel Callaway's girls, Fanny and Betsey. Betsey is sixteen, the other two fourteen," Butler said. "They were on the river in a canoe just below the fort when the Indians got them."

Ma put her hand to her cheek. "Poor things."

Pa asked if anyone else was having trouble.

Butler nodded. "Yup. You know about Hinkston's Station over on the Licking River north of here? It's just a few cabins. Well, they were attacked by about thirty Shawnee. Those families left the settlement and moved over to McClellan's Station on Elkhorn Creek," he said. "The folks at Leestown moved to McClellan's too. Same trouble."

"We haven't seen anything over this way," Pa said. "No sign of Indians at all."

"Well, I came to warn you." Butler got up. "Harrod says you're to come into Harrodsburg if you have any trouble. The folks over on Dick's River are talking about bringing in the women and children." He picked up his rifle and headed toward the door.

"Will you stay the night?" Ma asked him.

"No, ma'am. Got to go," Butler said. "Don't worry none about me. I can see in the dark."

Pa and my uncles walked out into the black night with him. Ma and I looked at each other. This was the worst possible news.

After that night, we were more watchful. Either Pa or Billy or Joe was close by us at all times. But after several weeks of no trouble with Indians, we got careless.

One day, Pa and my uncles were off clearing more land for crops, not too far away. I could hear their axes working on the trees. Ma and I thought it would be a good idea to collect some walnuts and hickory nuts. They would be good eating in the winter.

I took the basket Ma had made for me in one hand and grabbed hold of Charley with the other. We were going just to the edge of the clearing where the nut trees were. Ma looked from side to side as we walked and turned to look behind her toward the cabin.

I started to whistle a tune. Charley tried to do it, but could only make *roo-roo* sort of noises. Ma smiled at him and patted his head.

It was a fine autumn day, and there were plenty of nuts on the ground. Charley and I plunked ourselves down in the dry leaves and started to pick up the nuts.

I was watching Charley pucker up his lips trying to whistle when I heard Ma suck in her breath. I looked up. She was facing toward the cabin. I noticed her hand clenched behind her back.

"Polly," she whispered fiercely. I could hardly hear her. "Quick. Take Charley into the forest and run for Harrodsburg." Her hand unclenched and flapped at me.

"What is it?" The leaves rustled as I made a move to rise up.

"Quiet as you can," Ma hissed at me. "Run away. Now!"

"Ma?" I was real scared.

The hand behind her back made a motion for me to go. "I'll be right behind you. Take care of Charley," she whispered. "Go!" She never did turn around to look at us.

I grabbed my basket and Charley's hand and ran straight into the forest away from Ma. Charley could feel my fright, and he didn't make a sound, thank the Lord. I was pulling on him hard and half dragging him as we ran. The nuts came flying out of the basket. I didn't look back. Ma would be right behind us like she said.

After a while, I got worried about going in the wrong direction. But when I saw some familiar big rocks, I knew this was the way to Harrodsburg. There was only a mile or so more to run. Charley's face was all pulled back as he struggled to keep up. His feet were bleeding. Just as he looked up at me and our eyes met for a second, we heard a shot back yonder. It made both of us jerk. For a moment my breakfast almost came up.

I didn't know what to think. I just kept hearing Ma say, "I'll be right behind you. I'll be right behind you." I didn't look back.

Finally, we could see Harrodsburg. The stockade was almost finished. At first, I couldn't see where the gate was, and I started to panic and yell. As we ran across the clearing, some folks rushed out of the gate to meet us.

I couldn't speak, and Charley was crying too hard to say anything. A man, James Harrod I think it was, carried Charley into the stockade. I stumbled along behind him.

"It's the McBee children," I heard Harrod say.

I pulled at his sleeve. "Ma told us to run," I cried. "She's right behind us."

There was a lot of talking and yelling among the folks. Then Harrod and other men got on their horses and rode out the gate the way we came. I sat on the ground with my arm around Charley. My other arm hugged my basket.

A woman with dark hair came over with a rag and a bucket of water. She bent down and washed the blood off our bare feet. "Come get some food," she said.

But I pushed her away and said, "No. I've got to wait for Ma."

I went back to the open gate and looked out. Charley was hanging on to my skirt. The men were gone into the forest. Ma was nowhere in sight. Then, with a heavy heart, I saw smoke rising up from the direction of our place.

As time passed, my brother started to fidget. The same little slave boy we saw before came up to him. He pulled out a piece of wood he'd been cutting on and showed it to Charley. I let the boys go off together. I would wait for Ma alone.

That dark-haired woman came to stand next to me. She put her hand above her eyes to block the sun and looked out. For as long as she stood there watching the smoke in the sky, she didn't talk. I wanted her to go away.

It was nearing sunset, hours later, when I saw horses coming.

As they got closer, I could see Pa. He had Uncle Joe slung over the back of the horse. And there were Uncle Billy and Mr. Harrod. But I couldn't see Ma.

They rode in the gate, and Pa got off his horse as soon as he saw me. "Where's Charley?" he asked.

"He's here, Pa," I said. "Where's Ma?"

He put his hands on my shoulders. "It's mighty hard to tell you this, girl."

My body got hard as a board. I felt like I was going to be hit.

"She didn't make it," Pa said. "The Indians killed her."

My blood ran cold and I started to shake. "Did you bring her with you?" I asked.

Pa shook his head. "It was bad, Polly. We thought it best to bury her there."

"Oh Lord," I screamed. "Oh Lord."

"Pull yourself together now," Pa said as he hugged me to him. I buried my face against his buckskins. "Joe's been shot. Let's go tend to him."

That night they put Charley and me under some blankets in the sleeping loft of a cabin. I don't remember if we had food or not. Ma was dead. The cows had been shot. The cabin was gone, Uncle Billy told me, burned to the ground. Uncle Joe was moaning from the wound in his leg. I fell asleep clutching the basket Ma had made me.

III

A MARRIAGE

My children have tears in their eyes as they listen to my story. They feel sad every time I tell them how their granny died. Now I have to stop and wipe away my own tears. These days, it always makes me cry. But back then, at the time it happened, I couldn't even cry. My heart was hard.

* * *

I learned we were staying in the cabin of the dark-haired woman. Her name was Ellen McPeters. Uncle Billy told me she was a widow woman. Her husband was dead. It had happened a few months ago, when he was out hunting. When he didn't come back to the fort, folks went out to look for him. They found his body in the woods. He'd been shot and scalped by Indians. Uncle Billy told me to make myself helpful to Ellen and to watch Joe. He and Pa were going to our place to see what they could save.

Ellen McPeters scraped some bark from the slippery elm tree to put on Joe's wound. "I'll do it," I told her and grabbed it from her. I was feeling as mad as a bothered bear.

Later I went out to look around the fort.

"Your ma is the one that got killed," a girl said to me. I turned away, but she pulled on my arm.

19

"I'm sorry," she said. "My first ma died way back. I got a new ma now."

The girl was about my age. I should be friendly, I thought. "I'm Polly McBee. What's your name?" I asked her.

"Nancy Cross. I'm staying here while our fort is being built." She tugged at her hair and pointed. "Logan's Fort over by Dick's River. About twenty miles that way."

I showed her the direction in which our cabin had been.

"Look here," Nancy said. "Maybe you'll get a new ma."

"I don't want one," I told her. "Let's talk about something else."

Many families and slaves had come into the stockade for safety. Everyone was busy. Nancy and I soon found work to do. And we had a good gossip about the girls who had been taken from Boonesborough. Nancy told me that Betsey Callaway had married one of the men who saved her from the Indians. Nancy thought it was lovely, just like a story folks tell. As we carried water from the spring to the McPeters cabin, she babbled away like a turkey hen.

I got off badly with Ellen McPeters that day. When I came back to the cabin, she was holding my basket.

"Let it be," I said. "My ma gave that to me."

Ellen handed over the basket and said, "There are some things in there you may need." Then she turned to her cooking.

In the basket were a shawl and some shoes. With winter coming soon, I'd need them for warmth. I had forgotten that all my things were burned up. Although I felt bad about being so mean, I just couldn't find it in my heart to thank her. I didn't want her taking care of me anyway. I could fend for myself.

Later that night, Ellen passed me her Bible and asked me to read a verse or two. Lord forgive me, I almost threw it at her. Instead, I rested it on the bench and went up the ladder to the sleeping loft. Didn't she know I couldn't read?

I snuggled up against Charley and tried to sleep. Powerful feelings were storming around inside of me. Why did we ever leave Pennsylvania? Why did Ma die? I felt so alone and angry.

Pa and Uncle Billy came back from our place. They brought the cornmeal and the corn from the field. They even found one of the hogs in the woods, but that's all that was left. The Indians had carried off the iron pots. Everything else was burned — our cabin, our clothes, and all of Ma's things.

The weeks passed. Uncle Joe was mending. I worked hard and tried not to think about Ma all the time. Ellen took me to Jane Coomes, who said she was a teacher. Maybe I could help her when she taught the little ones to read. Sometimes the children didn't want to sit still, Jane Coomes said. So I said I would help. While watching the others, I learned the ABC's real quick. It was my secret.

One wintery day in early December, Nancy came running up to me. It was soap-making day. I was outside stirring the pot full of grease and lye. Charley and his friend were watching the fire under the pot, putting sticks on the fire when needed.

"You'll never guess," Nancy said as she caught her breath.

"I'll never guess what?" I asked.

"Mrs. Logan is having her baby. Didn't you hear her hollering?"

I looked up from the soap pot and listened. There was so much going on in the stockade that I had to listen hard. There were chickens clucking and dogs barking, and I could hear the blacksmith pounding on iron. Several young children were screeching away. On the far side of the stockade, I could see both white and black women gathered outside one of the cabins.

"Is she over there?" I asked Nancy.

"Yup. I'll go see what's happening," she said and was off as quick as a cat.

Ellen had come over to see how the soap was coming when Nancy returned and said, "She's hollering again." I saw a shadow cross Ellen's face as she questioned the girl about Mrs. Logan.

"My ma says she's doing good," said Nancy.

Nancy about wore her feet down running back and forth and delivering her news — "Not yet" and "Can't be long now" and "Pretty soon" and finally, "It's a boy."

Later in the day, I went over to see the baby. Lots of folks were in and out of the cabin to have a look. I peeked at him sleeping on the bed. It was a good-looking little fellow named William. Nancy smiled as if she had done the job herself.

The end of 1776 was coming on. One day Pa told me to come with him to bring in Ellen's cow for milking. Under a gray sky, we walked out of the stockade to find it. Pa said he had a surprise for me.

"This family needs a woman," he began. "I'm going to marry Ellen McPeters." Before I could speak, Pa pointed and said, "Get that cow, Polly."

I ran over to the cow and drove it back toward him.

"I can take care of us, Pa," I told him, hoping that he wouldn't marry that woman.

As he guided the cow toward the gate, Pa said, "That would be too hard on you."

He shushed me up and wouldn't listen to any more about it. They were married in the cabin that night. A man spoke some Bible words over them and said they were man and wife. Just like that, Ellen McPeters took our name and became Ellen McBee.

What I was feeling must have showed in my face. I was thinking that Nancy would probably say it was like a story folks tell. Well, this marriage was real. And I didn't like it one bit. Uncle Joe pulled me aside and sat me down.

"You need a talking to, girl," he said. This was from Joe who never did have much to say.

He rubbed the healed wound on his leg and went on. "You're just like me. Pigheaded and hardhearted."

A squirrel could have nested in my mouth, it dropped open so wide. I wasn't like Joe at all, and I told him so.

"Yes, you are," he said. "You're hanging on to what's past, and you're turning sour. It won't do to live that way." He thumped his chest. "I ought to know."

Suddenly I thought about Ma. My eyes flicked over to where my basket sat. Hadn't Ma said something about the past? Then my stomach churned and I thought, Oh Ma.

"Are you listening?" Joe asked. He had been saying something I didn't hear.

"What?"

"You need to let go," he said. "Can you do that?"

But I just hung my head. I couldn't make any sense out of what Uncle Joe was saying.

"Ellen is a fine woman," said Joe.

I scowled at him. "She's not like Ma."

"You're right, Polly. She's not. She's like herself."

Ellen looked at me across the cabin and smiled. I got up and ran right out the door. I stood in the cold by myself. I didn't think I was pigheaded and hardhearted. I just wanted my ma.

The next day, James Harrod came rushing into the stockade and told us about an Indian attack up near the Blue Licks. Two men were dead, two more captured. He feared the Indians were on the way to Harrodsburg.

IV

BLOODY SEVENS

Then it was 1777, the terrible year of the sevens.

I was at the stockade spring one day when I saw Simon Butler ride in the gate and go to the blockhouse where Harrod lived. Soon after, there was a stir among the men. Pa headed over to the cabin. I dropped the bucket I was filling and hurried after him.

When I entered the cabin, Pa was saying, "McClellan's Station has been attacked by a large group of Indians. There's one dead and three wounded, including McClellan himself. Butler says the Indians headed north across the Ohio River, so the fort should be safe for now."

"What are we going to do?" Uncle Billy asked.

"We're riding up to the river with Harrod," Pa answered. "George Clark is back from the east with 500 pounds of gunpowder."

Uncle Joe said, "We surely do need it."

"We're going to go get that gunpowder now," Pa told them. "So get your rifles and saddle up."

Ellen and I stood at the gate and watched them ride out — James Harrod, Simon Butler, Pa and my uncles, and many other men. They might meet with great danger, but the gunpowder was so important to us that they had to go get it. Without gunpowder we couldn't protect ourselves at the fort.

All of us were scared that January. When Pa returned, he told us that everyone knew the Indians would be back. Folks from the outlying stations were streaming into Harrodsburg. They couldn't stay out there by themselves because the Indians would get them. By the end of the month, the folks from McClellan's came in too, leaving their place empty. They said that John McClellan had died from his wounds.

There was a lot of talk about leaving Kentucky. Pa said our family absolutely was not going back east, and Billy and Joe agreed. The McBees would stay and fight. But many folks packed up and headed back to Virginia where they had come from. There was so much coming and going, it made me dizzy.

We were preparing for attack. We started keeping the cows and horses in the stockade every night. When we went out to get firewood, men with rifles went along. Women were melting lead for making bullets. Children were hauling buckets of water to put in sleeping lofts. This was in case Indians shot fire arrows at the cabin roofs. The water would be used to put out the fires.

Ellen showed me how to load a rifle. She said it was something every woman should know, to help her man when the attack came. The rifle was almost five feet long, just about my size. I had to stand up to load it. First, I learned to pour some gunpowder down the end of the rifle. Then I put a little patch of cloth over the end of the rifle and set a bullet on the patch. I had to use both hands to push the bullet and patch all the way in with a stick called a ramrod. Then I put some gunpowder into the lock and cocked the lock. Now it was ready to hand over for firing. It took men about a minute to completely reload. It must have taken all of ten minutes for me to do it. Ellen said that I would get better. That ruffled my feathers. I said no doubt I would.

I was still acting mean to Ellen. Not that she did anything to deserve it. She was helpful and taught me things, but it just made me spitting mad every time. Uncle Joe said he was giving up on me. And Uncle Billy gave me plenty of room.

It was in February that Nancy told me she was leaving. Logan's fort was finished. Nancy's family and several others

were moving there. When the horses were packed up and ready to go, Charley and I went to see her off.

"I wish you didn't have to go," I said. I'd miss Nancy something terrible, even her constant chattering.

"We're friends forever, aren't we, Polly?"

"Oh, yes."

She gave me a hug. Then she grabbed Charley and gave him a big kiss on the cheek.

Charley rubbed his cheek and whined, "Don't do that."

The horses started moving out the gate. Mrs. Logan was carrying her new baby wrapped in a blanket. Nancy looked for her own family and ran over to them. As they walked across the clearing, she turned back and yelled, "I'll get a letter to you." Then they disappeared into the forest.

The rest of February was so quiet we didn't know what to think. I went on helping Jane Coomes at her school. It gave me a chance to learn some words. If Nancy got someone to bring a letter, I wanted to be able to make sense of it. I also learned my numbers and could write 1777 in the dirt.

Then it was March, and the end of peace.

Two groups of men were out. One group was up to Shawnee Spring making maple sugar. The other was over to the empty Hinkston's Station to get flax, which was needed for making clothes.

Late that afternoon, James Ray from the sugar camp came running into the clearing, hollering that the men had been attacked. The alarm spread quickly. Those of us who had been outside the stockade ran in, and the gate was closed.

Jane Coomes cried, "Where's William?"

"Oh Lord. I don't know," Ray said, trying to catch his breath. He had run four miles. "There were about seventy Shawnee with their chief, Black Fish. They got my brother."

The men started arguing about what to do. In the end, it was decided that thirty men should ride out to see if any of the Ray party were still alive. Harrod and George Clark led the way. Pa remained with the others to protect the fort. I stayed with Jane

Coomes until the men returned. William Coomes came back un-harmed. He had hidden in a tree to save himself, but two men had been killed.

"I saw them kill William Ray," he said. "Even after the Indians left, I was too scared to move."

"More men coming," someone yelled. And the gates were opened to let in the men who had gone for the flax. I had to get out of the way as folks crowded closer to hear the news. By now everyone in the fort was gathered around.

"There were Shawnee in the empty cabins at Hinkston's," a man shouted. "On the way back we saw signs of a large war party. A couple hundred Indians."

Another man said that Simon Butler had taken off to warn the folks at Boonesborough.

As the darkness settled in, we knew that Indians were coming soon. There were places between some of the cabins where the stockade wasn't finished, so a cane bonfire was lighted. We worked through the cold night to close the gaps in the wall. Holes were dug and logs were cut to stand in them. I wasn't of much help, but I held Pa's ax when he rested and ran off to get things for Billy and Joe when they asked me to.

There were only one hundred twenty-one men in all of Ken-tucky who could fight — at Harrodsburg where we were, at Boonesborough, and at Logan's Fort. We were two hundred miles from the next folks in Virginia and Pennsylvania. And now there were a few hundred Indians ready to come and get us. We prayed hard as we worked that night.

At dawn, I went into the cabin looking for Charley and found him asleep before the fire. Ellen put a wooden bowl of corn and milk on the table for me.

"Any sign of Indians?" she asked.

I yawned and stretched as I sat down. "I don't think so," I said. After eating, I put my head down on the table and was soon fast asleep.

I jerked awake some time later when I heard hollering outside the cabin. Ellen and Charley were gone. Throwing a shawl around

my shoulders, I ran out. Everyone was over on one side of the stockade, and smoke was rising up in the distance. I peeked through a chink in the stockade and saw an empty cabin smoking in the clearing. I heard the gate open. A group of men were going out to take a look. I watched through my peekhole as they crouched low and ran.

The men reached the cabin and seemed to be looking around. Suddenly, shots rang out from the woods. The men returned the shots and bent to reload.

Shots were fired from other directions, and I saw Shawnee begin to step into the clearing. Inside the fort, some men were running for the blockhouses to shoot from the second floors. Others shot through portholes in the stockade walls. Suddenly Ellen was beside me. She grabbed my arm and hauled me over to where Pa and Billy and Joe were firing. Pa stood on a tree stump to shoot over the top of the stockade. Under the stormy winter sky we kept the rifles loaded as Pa and Billy and Joe took shot after shot.

"The men are trying to come in," Joe shouted. "Cover them."

Pa hollered, "There must be a hundred Indians out there."

The wind picked up and blew sharp pieces of snow in my face. My shawl kept blowing off. It was freezing cold. Ellen noticed me and handed over a hot rifle. She told me to warm my hands a moment. Then she grabbed it back and poured in the gunpowder.

"Oh Lord," I heard Billy yell. "One of the fellows is trying to scalp an Indian. Is he plumb crazy?"

We kept it up all day as the storm grew worse and worse. I sank to the ground to try and keep warm. Charley was hanging onto me as I handed over gunpowder, a bullet and a patch, and the ramrod to Ellen again and again. By late afternoon, there was a howling storm. Finally, the firing stopped.

Uncle Billy carried me back to the cabin and put me at the hearth. "It's a wonder you're not frozen," he said. "Now warm yourself up." I fell asleep in the warm glow of the fire.

V

THE SHAWNEE

I walked out in the snow the next day to have a look at the dead Indian who'd been killed, scalped, and dragged into the fort for all to see. So that's what it looks like, I thought. It made my stomach roll over.

Folks were saying that most of the Indians had gone far into the forest. Only a few stayed near Harrodsburg to shoot at anyone who went out the gate. Everyone was worried about food. It was decided that groups of men should go out to get the corn left at the empty stations.

Uncle Billy and Uncle Joe were arguing. "There's not enough food," Billy was saying. "I'm going out to hunt."

"There are Indians out there," Joe said.

Billy scratched his head. "Well, someone's got to do it."

"I never did see such a fool," Joe said over his shoulder as he walked away. "At least wait until dark."

James Ray came up to Billy. "I'm going to hunt too," he said. He was only seventeen.

"It sure is good to meet another fool," Billy said and slapped Ray on the back. They shared a hearty laugh.

They did gallop out into the darkness, but not together. Each went his separate way, and came back the next night with buffalo meat for the rest of us. Other men, along with Pa and Uncle Joe, went out in the daytime like a small army to visit the empty stations. On each trip, they'd get the corn from the corncribs and rush back to the safety of the stockade. And each time, I could hear the rifle shots of the Indians hiding at the edge of the clearing. The rest of us stayed inside the fort. Only the falling snow and rain marked the passing of days. The sun didn't come out even once.

On March 18, the Shawnee came back again. One of our men was outside the stockade when the Indians burst from the woods. He was killed and scalped in the clearing. His family was watching from inside. They saw it happen.

Again, Ellen and I reloaded the rifles for Pa and my uncles. Under heavy black storm clouds, the attack went on for hours. Finally, the Indians went back into the woods. Only the one man was killed that day. Ellen went over to his cabin to comfort the family.

We had several days of rain, and then the temperature dropped way below freezing. It was hard to get warm. The best thing to do was stay inside the cabin. Men who weren't out hunting or getting corn crowded into the top story of the blockhouses and kept watch. For about ten days it was quiet.

The cattle and horses were a big problem. There wasn't anything for them to eat in the stockade. Usually they'd feed out in the cornfields. Finally, some armed men took a few cows and horses out to graze. That was March 28.

I was in the cabin when the first shots fired, and I heard the alarm raised. I ran to the stockade wall to look through. There were Indians everywhere, well over a hundred. They were shooting the cows and running off with the horses as our men fired from the fort. The men outside raced madly for the gate. One man fell down like a sack of cornmeal, shot dead. Then another fell, and the Indians carried him off. The other two men reached the gate and squeezed in.

I couldn't find Pa and Uncle Joe. Uncle Billy, I knew, had gone out hunting last night and would be far away by now. I found Charley huddled on the ground with his hands over his ears, and I yanked him up as I ran past.

Ellen was nowhere to be seen, and the cabin was empty. Oh Lord, I thought. What do I do now?

Charley and I ran out again. Folks were running every which way. My eyes scanned the walls of the fort, but Pa wasn't there. Then I dragged Charley over to one of the blockhouses and went in. The rifle shots from the men upstairs made an awful noise. I went up the ladder to the room above. Ellen was there reloading as Pa and Uncle Joe peered out the small windows into the clearing. She motioned me to come over.

"The Indians are shooting fire arrows," she hollered in my ear. "Go back to the cabin and watch for fire."

I stared at her. I wanted to stay with Pa. "Go," she ordered and gave me a push. I ran to the cabin with Charley.

The buckets of water were up in the sleeping loft. If the roof caught fire, I'd have to use them to put the fire out. From inside I couldn't tell what was happening, so Charley and I stayed outside the cabin to watch the roof. I made him run from one side to the other and tell me if he saw any fire. "No," he said as he checked one side. "No," he said as he checked the other. I put my face in my hands and said, "Oh Lord, I don't know how to do this."

"Polly! Polly!" Charley was pulling on my skirt. "The chimney."

I looked up at it. There was an arrow sticking in the chimney, and flames were shooting up its side. Our chimney was made of wood, packed with mud on the inside. Chimney fires happened quite a bit, and we kept a long pole handy in case we had to pull the chimney down fast.

I grabbed the 12-foot pole. It was heavy and hard to handle. At first, it tipped me over backwards.

"Hurry, Polly," Charley was hollering.

I picked that pole right up again and started banging it against the chimney. But the wood wouldn't break up. Now the fire was getting higher up the chimney and was licking against the cabin roof. I rested a moment. Then I used the pole again to poke at the wood chimney until sticks of burning wood started breaking loose. Charley beat on the sticks as they fell to put out the flames.

"Watch your head, Charley," I screamed at him as more wood came crashing down. Finally the whole chimney tipped over, just missing us both. We stomped on the sticks until the fires were out. We had saved the cabin.

The chimney was rebuilt the next day. Pa kept saying that I was a wonder. He was real proud of Charley, who strutted around telling all the folks what he had done. I thought he sounded just like Uncle Billy. Ellen thanked me, but I was mean to her as usual. I couldn't seem to stop it.

The days went on and on. There was never enough food. Our clothes started to look pretty bad, but there wasn't enough flax or buffalo wool to spin. Spring flowers bloomed in the dirt next to our cabin, and the weather warmed. Except for our brave men who went out for wood, corn, or game, we stayed in the stockade. On April 29, the Indians returned, and another man was killed. The next day, Simon Butler stopped in to see how folks were doing. Everyone gathered round.

"Boonesborough was hit bad last week," he told us. "One's dead. Captain Boone and three others are wounded. The Indians haven't attacked Logan's Fort yet. But they're lurking around."

Butler turned his head as if he were looking for someone. "Where's that Polly McBee?" he asked.

I pushed through the crowd. "That's me," I said.

"Well, I got a mighty important letter for you." Butler handed me a piece of folded paper. "A young girl at Logan's almost talked my ear off, telling me about you."

"That's Nancy," I said. "Is she all right?"

"If the amount of talking she can do is any sign," he laughed, "I'd say she's just fine."

After thanking Simon Butler, I ran off to try and read the letter. The first word was "Polly." I could make sense of my name. Then she wrote, "I am not dead. Love, Nancy." I could read it! Jane Coomes let me use her quill pen to write back. "Nancy," I wrote, "It is bad here." I knew a few words. Then I signed it with my name. "Polly." It was the first time I ever did write on paper. Butler said he would take the letter back to Logan's fort.

In May, some armed men and slaves sneaked out to plant the corn. Indians were seen nearly every day around the fort, but there was no big attack. We did hear that Boonesborough had two days of attack, and Logan's was hit at the end of the month.

It all came falling down on me in June. We'd been in the stockade for months. I was still angry and mean and just couldn't shake that awful feeling. I didn't want Ellen to be close to me at all, but I didn't know why.

One night at supper, Pa said that old Barney Stagner had been killed outside the fort. The Indians had cut off his head. It was so dreadful and so terrible that a silence fell at the table. I looked up. Everyone had a sickly look on their face. There was too much danger and death for anyone to bear. That's when it hit me.

I jumped up. "Where's my basket?" I said. "Where's my basket?" I found it and hugged it to me. Oh, I didn't want to let myself think of it. Ma was really dead! The Shawnee had killed her too. "It can't be," I cried. But I knew it was. I had to face it.

Then a big howl came out of my mouth, and I fell to the floor weeping. "Oh, Ma," I sobbed.

Ellen bent down and pulled me up. Making sure I had the basket in my hand, she hugged me to her and let me cry. Then Pa took me in his lap. I buried my face against him as I sobbed and sobbed. "Let it out, girl," he said, patting my back. "Let go of it."

All my sadness poured out. I think my heart started to heal itself that night.

VI

A NEW LIFE

I remembered what Ma had told me before she was killed. She said that it's no good pining for things in the past. I should take my heart with me into the present. That was why she made the basket to remind me. I came to understand that Ma was part of my past. Although I still loved her, I had to go on. So I put my heart in the basket like she said.

I don't mean to say that I got happy all at once. But the anger left me suddenly. It was hard to remember why I had felt that way. I think the pain of losing Ma had twisted up my insides and made my heart hard. Now it was softer, but I felt as empty as a bucket with a hole in it.

Just like the gate of my heart, one day in August the gate of the stockade was opened. The women and children were allowed to go out for a short time. We could hardly believe it.

Some army men from Virginia had arrived to help us. With the extra armed men, they thought it would be safe to let us out. The Indians had pulled back into the woods and maybe had gone home. The army must have scared them.

"It's mighty good to be out," said Ellen as we passed through the gate.

"Are the Indians gone?" I asked, nervously looking around. Ellen gave me a gentle push to keep me moving.

"Don't worry yourself," she said. "Let the riflemen watch for Indians. Just enjoy it."

Charley and his friend were running and whooping like wild beasts. They had no trouble enjoying themselves.

I let the long, fresh grass tickle my hand as I walked away from the gate. The sunshine on my face felt a heap better than it did inside the stockade. Isn't that peculiar, I thought, the sun is the same both places. Maybe it was because we felt so cooped up when we were inside. There were purple and yellow wild flowers all around, and I bent to pick a few.

"Polly?" It was Ellen. I turned to face her. "I'm going to have a baby," she said and waited for me to say something.

I looked everywhere but at her. A baby, I thought. I didn't feel a thing about it, no happiness or anger. I just felt empty. "Oh," I said. She stared at me for a bit and walked away.

I was always to remember that lovely day outside as the day I heard about the baby. Some time after that, the Virginia men left, and the Indians came back to lurk in the woods beyond the clearing. We were closed in the fort again.

"Jane Coomes tells me you're smart as a whip," Uncle Billy said to me one night in the cabin. "Read us some Bible verses, girl."

I had been working hard at learning to read all kinds of words. Jane Coomes was right pleased with me, and I was ready to show off. Ellen got the Bible out.

This was the first time I had looked in Ellen's Bible. I opened the cover and saw handwriting on the inside. It said her name, when she was born, and when she was married to the man before Pa. Under that writing was the name Polly and the years 1775-1776. My Lord, I thought, she had a baby named like me. The little girl died when she was only a year old.

"Keep going, Polly," Pa said. "Find a good verse to read to us."

I looked at Ellen, who sat there with tears in her eyes. She nodded at me and smiled. She knew I had read about her Polly.

A sudden warm feeling struck me. I liked Ellen!

I read a good many verses from the Bible that night. Some

words I didn't know, but no one seemed to pay much mind. As I was reading, I smiled for the first time since Ma had died. The Lord's love just filled me up. Uncle Joe noticed and said, "That sour look is gone for good."

That's when I started living again. I'm not saying that things were better all round. The Indians were a great danger to us, and our supplies were short. We knew now that the Indians were working for the British. In Kentucky and all along the frontier back east, the Indians attacked where the British told them to. We were a part of the big war for independence after all. We talked about the time when all the trouble would be over. That's when we said, "The good times are coming, but we may never live to see them." Oh my, yes, we were still in danger.

As winter came again, I started work on a birthing present for Ellen. It would be a basket like the one Ma made for me. I must have started three or four of them before I got it right. Finally, I was happy with the basket and couldn't wait for the baby to be born.

It was on a December day when Ellen told me her baby was coming. She sent me out for Jane Coomes to come and help. When we got back to the cabin, Ellen was lying in the bed.

"Stay with me, Polly," she said. "I want you to be here."

"I will." I was real scared, but Jane didn't looked worried. Nancy would love this, I thought. I remembered her running back and forth when Mrs. Logan had her baby.

"What was your Polly like?" I asked as I sat down close to the bed.

"She was a pretty little baby. Her hair was sandy-yellow like yours," Ellen told me. Then her face pulled back in pain for a moment. "When I first saw you, that's what I thought. That you reminded me of my girl. It seemed right that you were called Polly too."

"I was so mean to you," I said. "Can you forgive me?"

She patted my hand. "There's no need. I know what it's like to lose your loved ones."

The time passed, and her pains got worse. Jane Coomes was

frowning now. She told me to leave the cabin for a spell.

It had started to snow. Pa, Uncle Billy, and Uncle Joe were standing outside waiting to hear what was happening. Charley was trying to stand just like Billy with his hip slung out.

"Nothing yet," I said.

"Shucks," said Uncle Billy. "It's the waiting that makes a man crazy."

Uncle Joe glared at him. "She's not even your wife, Billy."

"When are *you* getting married?" Pa asked Billy with a grin.

Billy shrugged, "I like my freedom too much."

"No woman would have you, more likely," Joe said without cracking a smile. But he made the rest of us laugh.

"I'd better be getting back." I left them out in the snow. They looked like sad hound dogs standing there.

"There's some trouble," Jane Coomes told me when I came in. "Come hold her hand."

It took a terrible long time. Sometimes Ellen hollered out and squeezed my hand tightly. Then she'd lie so still I thought she was dying.

"Keep trying," I said to her.

Finally the baby was born, a little girl. After cleaning up, I knelt down to have a close look at the baby.

"She looks a little like Charley," I laughed. Then I gave Ellen the basket I made for her. There was no reason to tell her what a basket meant to me, that Ma had told me to carry my heart in it. I think Ellen already knew that.

"How pretty," Ellen said. "Just like yours." She looked at the little baby in her arms. "Since you gave the first present, why don't you pick a name for her?"

"Would Abby be a good name?" I asked. "That's what my first ma was called."

"That would be lovely," Ellen said.

When Uncle Billy saw Abby, he said she looked red and scrawny. Pa gave him a poke. Uncle Joe took a quick look and seemed embarassed. Charley gave Ellen a kiss and asked if Abby wanted to play with him. Pa looked right proud of the baby, and

he gave Ellen a big smile.

When I had the time, I sat down to write another letter to my friend. "Dear Nancy. I love my new ma. We have a baby girl. Love, Polly."

That was the end of the year of the sevens. We'd seen a lot of death, but there was new life too.

* * *

"Now tell us about the Indian trouble that followed," my own girl said. The end of 1777 hadn't been the end of our struggle. We were in danger for many more years. The war went on and on. My children knew these stories too.

"Or tell about 1779," my other daughter begged me, "when you met Pa. About how he thought you were plumb pretty. And he decided to marry you the first time he saw you. Please."

I looked at the cabin wall behind my children. Hanging there was the basket that I still kept. I thought of the day when Ma had died, and my eyes filled with tears. Telling this story always took a lot out of me.

"No," I said and stood up. "That's enough for now."

AMERICA'S PAST

The Frontier During the Revolution

*In 1777, the Americans are fight-
ing the British. It is the time of the
Revolutionary War.*

*The red area on the map shows
where the Americans live. Only a few
brave pioneers live over the Appala-
chian Mountains at Boonesborough,
Harrodsburg, and Logan's Fort. They
are surrounded by Indian tribes.
Farther west and north are British
forts (shown by blue dots).*

THE BORDER WAR

*In the 1770s, many people in the thirteen colonies wanted to
be free from British control. On July 4, 1776, the Americans declared their independence. Since 1775 , the British armies had
been attacking along the east coast. They fought first in the north
— in Massachusetts, Rhode Island, New York, Pennsylvania, and
New Jersey. General George Washington led the American armies.
Later, there were battles farther south in Virginia, the Carolinas,
and Georgia.*

*The war came to the western frontier too. All along the
western border from New York to Georgia, the British sent the
Indians to fight the frontier families. This was called the Border
War. The few settlers who lived on the other side of the Appala-
chian Mountains were in great danger as well. They lived within
three small stockades in Kentucky, which was then a county
belonging to Virginia.*

46

In the north the Iroquois, Mingo, Wyandot, Delaware, and Shawnee Indians raided settlements along the border. The British asked tribes along the Great Lakes to join the war too. Cherokee and Creek Indians raided southern settlements.

Kentucky had no Indian villages. But the Indians to the north and south used this area as a hunting ground. The land south of the Ohio River was rich with buffalo and deer. When the first American settlers came to Kentucky, the Indians were angry. They didn't want settlers on their hunting ground. It was easy for the British to convince the Indians to fight the Kentucky pioneers.

Some Kentucky men wore a complete outfit made of buckskin.

The people in Kentucky lived through great hardship. They needed to be strong and brave. Much of the time, they had to remain inside the stockades. Getting enough food was a constant struggle. The Shawnee and other Indians attacked again and again during the war. Many of the pioneers were killed. Women lost their husbands, and many children were orphaned.

The United States won its independence when a treaty was signed in 1783. In the east, the war was over. But now all the land from the Atlantic Ocean to the Mississippi River was claimed by the Americans. So the Indians were still angry, and they continued to fight along the frontier. In Kentucky, the Indian attacks went on until well into the 1790s.

A girl living in Kentucky, like Polly in this story, could have spent almost her whole life in danger of Indian attack.

To survive on the frontier, pioneers needed a good gun like this Kentucky rifle.